Parents and Caregivers,

Stone Arch Readers are designed to provide enjoyable reading experiences, as well as opportunities to develop vocabulary, literacy skills, and comprehension. Here are a few ways to support your beginning reader:

- Talk with your child about the ideas addressed in the story.

- Discuss each illustration, mentioning the characters, where they are, and what they are doing.

- Read with expression, pointing to each word. You may want to read the whole story through and then revisit parts of the story to ensure that the meanings of words or phrases are understood.

- Talk about why the character did what he or she did and what your child would do in that situation.

- Help your child connect with characters and events in the story.

Remember, reading with your child should be fun, not forced. Each moment spent reading with your child is a priceless investment in his or her literacy life.

Gail Saunders-Smith, Ph.D.

STONE ARCH READERS

are published by Stone Arch Books, a Capstone Imprint
1710 Roe Crest Drive
North Mankato, Minnesota 56003
www.capstonepub.com

Library of Congress Cataloging-in-Publication Data
Crow, Melinda Melton.
Brave Fire Truck / by Melinda Melton Crow ; illustrated by Chad Thompson.
p. cm. — (Stone Arch readers. Wonder wheels)
Audience: Ages 4-6.
Summary: "Fire Truck is very brave, and while he is off fighting a fire, School Bus, Tractor,
and Train await his return"—Provided by publisher.
ISBN 978-1-4342-3029-4 (library binding) — ISBN 978-1-4342-3384-4 (pbk.)
1. Fire engines—Juvenile fiction. 2. School buses—Juvenile fiction. 3. Tractors—Juvenile fiction.
4. Railroad trains—Juvenile fiction. [1. Fire engines—Fiction. 2. School buses—Fiction. 3. Tractors—
Fiction. 4. Railroad trains—Fiction.] I. Thompson, Chad, ill. II. Title.
PZ7.C88536Br 2011
[E]—dc22
                                                    2010050152

Reading Consultants:
Gail Saunders-Smith, Ph.D.
Melinda Melton Crow, M.Ed.
Laurie K. Holland, Media Specialist

Art Director: Kay Fraser
Designer: Hilary Wacholz
Production Specialist: Michelle Biedscheid

written by **Melinda Melton Crow**

illustrated by **Chad Thompson**

Printed in the United States of America in Stevens Point, Wisconsin.
052016   009764R

Brave
Fire Truck

STONE ARCH BOOKS
a capstone imprint

School Bus, Tractor, Fire Truck,
and Train are friends.

School Bus is in his garage.

Tractor is in his garage.

Train is in his garage.

Fire Truck is not in his garage.

"Where is Fire Truck?"
said Tractor.

"Fire Truck went to work"
said School Bus.

Fire Truck raced to the fire.

Fire Truck put out the fire.

Fire Truck went home.

"Here comes Fire Truck,"
said Tractor.

"You are so brave," said Train.

"It is my job to be brave,"
said Fire Truck.

"Way to go, Fire Truck!"

STORY WORDS

friends   raced   brave

garage   fire   job

Total Word Count: 89

STONE ARCH **READERS**   LEVEL 1

Lucky School Bus

written by
Melinda Melton Crow

illustrated by
Chad Thompson

STONE ARCH **READERS**   LEVEL 1

Busy Busy **Train**

written by
Melinda Melton Crow

illustrated by
Chad Thompson

STONE ARCH **READERS**   LEVEL 1

Brave Fire Truck

written by
Melinda Melton Crow

illustrated by
Chad Thompson

STONE ARCH **READERS**   LEVEL 1

Helpful Tractor

written by
Melinda Melton Crow

illustrated by
Chad Thompson